TAKE NOTICE!

This book belongs to

_____

_____

"*Presented
by* _____

_____

THE BROWNIES: THEIR BOOK

BY
PALMER COX

DOVER PUBLICATIONS, INC., NEW YORK

This Dover edition, first published in 1964, is an unabridged and unaltered republication of the work first published by The Century Company in 1887.

International Standard Book Number: 0-486-21265-3
Library of Congress Catalog Card Number: 64-25091

Manufactured in the United States of America

Dover Publications, Inc.
180 Varick Street
New York 14, N.Y.

BROWNIES, like fairies and goblins, are imaginary little sprites, who are supposed to delight in harmless pranks and helpful deeds. They work and sport while weary households sleep, and never allow themselves to be seen by mortal eyes.

CONTENTS.

ix

THE BROWNIES AT SCHOOL.

AS Brownies rambled 'round one night,
A country schoolhouse came in sight;
And there they paused awhile to speak
About the place, where through the week
The scholars came, with smile or whine,
Each morning at the stroke of nine.
"This is," said one, "the place, indeed,
Where children come to write and read.
'T is here, through rules and rods to suit,
The young idea learns to shoot;
And here the idler with a grin
In nearest neighbor pokes the pin,

Or sighs to break his scribbled slate
And spring at once to man's estate.
How oft from shades of yonder grove
I 've viewed at eve the shouting drove
As from the door they crowding broke,
Like oxen from beneath the yoke."

1

Another said: "The teacher's chair,
The ruler, pen, and birch are there;
The blackboard hangs against the wall;
The slate 's at hand, the books and all.
We might go in to read and write
And master sums like scholars bright."

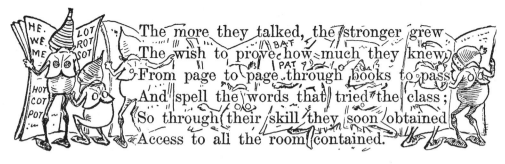

The more they talked, the stronger grew
The wish to prove how much they knew,
From page to page through books to pass,
And spell the words that tried the class;
So through their skill they soon obtained
Access to all the room contained.

"I 'll play," cried one, "the teacher's part;
I know some lessons quite by heart,
And every section of the land
To me is plain as open hand."
"With all respect, my friend, to you,"
Another said, "that would not do.
You 're hardly fitted, sir, to rule;
Your place should be the dunce's stool.
You 're not with great endowments
    blessed;
Besides, your temper 's not the best,
And those who train the budding mind
Should own a disposition kind.
The rod looks better on the tree
Than resting by the master's knee;
I 'll be the teacher, if you please;
I know the rivers, lakes, and seas,
And, like a banker's clerk, can throw
The figures nimbly in a row.
I have the patience, love, and grace,
So requisite in such a case."

Now some bent o'er a slate or book,
And some at blackboards station took.
They clustered 'round the globe with zeal,
And kept it turning like a wheel.

3

Said one, "I 've often heard it said,
The world is rounder than your head,
And here, indeed, we find it true.
With both the poles at once in view,
With latitudes and each degree
All measured out on land and sea."
Another said, "I thought I knew
The world from Maine to Timbuctoo,
Or could, without a guide, have found
My way from Cork to Puget Sound;
But here so many things I find
That never dawned upon my mind,
On sundry points, I blush to say,
I 've been a thousand miles astray."
"'T is like an egg," another cried,
"A little longer than it 's wide,
With islands scattered through the seas
Where savages may live at ease;

PALMER COX.

And buried up in Polar snows
You find the hardy Eskimos;
While here and there some scorching spots
Are set apart for Hottentots.
And see the rivers small and great,
That drain a province or a state;
The name and shape of every nation;
Their faith, extent, and population;
And whether governed by a King,
A President, or council ring."

While some with such expressions bold
Surveyed the globe as 'round it rolled,
Still others turned to ink and pen,
And, spreading like a brooding hen,
They scrawled a page to show the band
Their special " style," or " business hand."

The teacher had enough to do,
To act his part to nature true:
He lectured well the infant squad,
He rapped the desk and shook the rod,
And stood the dunce upon the stool,
A laughing-stock to all the school—
But frequent changes please the crowd,
So lengthy reign was not allowed;
And when one master had his hour,
Another took the rod of power;
And thus they changed to suit the case,
Till many filled the honored place.

So taken up was every mind
With fun and study well combined,

They noticed not the hours depart,
Until the sun commenced to dart
A sheaf of lances, long and bright,
Above the distant mountain height;
Then from the schoolroom, in a heap,
They jumped and tumbled, twenty deep,
In eager haste to disappear
In deepest shades of forests near.

6

When next the children gathered there,
With wondering faces fresh and fair,
It took an hour of morning prime,
According to the teacher's time,
To get the books in place once more,
And order to the room restore.
So great had been the haste to hide,
The windows were left open wide;
And scholars knew, without a doubt,
That Brownies had been thereabout.

THE BROWNIES' RIDE.

ONE night a cunning Brownie band
 Was roaming through a farmer's land,
And while the rogues went prying 'round,
The farmer's mare at rest they found;
And peeping through the stable-door,
They saw the harness that she wore.
The sight was tempting to the eye,
For there the cart was standing nigh.

"That mare," said one, "deserves her feed—
Believe me, she's no common breed;
Her grit is good: I've seen her dash
Up yonder slope without the lash,
 Until her load—a ton of hay—
 Went bouncing in beside the bay.
 In this same cart, old Farmer Gill
 Takes all his corn and wheat to mill;
 It must be strong, though rude and rough;
 It runs on wheels, and that's enough."

Now, Brownies seldom idle stand
When there's a chance for fun at hand.

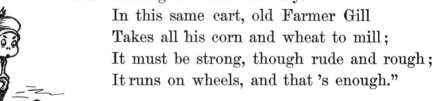

So plans were laid without delay;
The mare was dragged from oats and hay,
The harness from the peg they drew,
And every one to action flew.
It was a sight one should behold
To see them working, young and old;
Two wrinkled elves, like leather browned,
Whose beards descended near the ground,
Along with youngsters did their best
With all the ardor of the rest.

9

While some prepared a rein or trace,
Another slid the bit in place;
More buckled bands with all their might,
Or drew the harness close and tight.

When every strap a buckle found,
And every part was safe and sound,
Then 'round the cart the Brownies flew,—
The hardest task was yet to do.
It often puzzles bearded men,
Though o'er and o'er performed again.

Some held the shafts to steer them straight,
More did their best to balance weight,
While others showed both strength and art
In backing Mag into the cart.
At length the heavy job was done,
And horse and cart moved off as one.

Now down the road the gentle steed
Was forced to trot at greatest speed.
A merrier crowd than journeyed there
Was never seen at Dublin Fair.
Some found a seat, while others stood,
Or hung behind as best they could;
While many, strung along, astride,
Upon the mare enjoyed the ride.

The night was dark, the lucky elves
Had all the turnpike to themselves.
No surly keeper barred the way,
For use of road demanding pay,
Nor were they startled by the cry
Of robbers shouting, " Stand or die !"
Across the bridge and up the hill
And through the woods to Warren's mill,—
A lengthy ride, ten miles at least,—
Without a rest they drove the beast,
And then were loath enough to rein
Old Mag around for home again.

11

Nor was the speed, returning, slow;
The mare was more inclined to go,
Because the feed of oats and hay
Unfinished in her manger lay.
So through the yard she wheeled her load
As briskly as she took the road.
No time remained to then undo
The many straps which tight they drew,
For in the east the reddening sky
Gave warning that the sun was nigh.

The halter rope was  quickly wound
About the nearest post they found;
Then off they scam- pered, left and right,
And disappeared at once from sight.

When Farmer Gill that morning fair
Came out and viewed his jaded mare,
I may not here in verse repeat
His exclamations all complete.
He gnashed his teeth, and glared around,
And struck his fists, and stamped the ground,
And chased the dog across the farm,
Because it failed to give alarm.
"I 'd give a stack of hay," he cried,
"To catch the rogue who stole the ride!"
But still awry suspicion flew,—
Who stole the ride he never knew.

THE BROWNIES ON SKATES.

ONE night, when the cold moon hung low
    And winter wrapped the world in snow
    And bridged the streams in wood and field
With ice as smooth as shining shield,
    Some skaters swept
        in graceful style
The glistening surface,
    file on file.
For hours the Brownies
    viewed the show,
Commenting   on   the
    groups below;

PALMER COX

Said one: "That pleasure might be ours —
We have the feet and motive powers;
No mortal need us Brownies teach,
If skates were but within our reach."
Another answered: "Then, my friend,
To hear my plan let all attend.
I have a building in my mind
That we within an hour can find.

Three golden balls hang by the door,
Like oranges from Cuba's shore;
Behind the dusty counter stands
A native of queer, far-off lands;
The place is filled with various things,
From baby-carts to banjo-strings;

Here hangs a gun without a lock
Some Pilgrim bore to Plymouth rock;
And there a pair of goggles lie,
That saw the red-coats marching by;
While piles of club and rocker skates
Of every shape the buyer waits!
Though second-hand, I'm sure they'll do,
And serve our wants as well as new.
That place we'll enter as we may,
To-morrow night, and bear away
A pair, the best that come to hand,
For every member of the band."
At once, the enterprise so bold
Received support from young and old.

A place to muster near the town,
And meeting hour they noted down;
And then retiring for the night,
They soon were lost to sound and sight.

15

When evening next her visit paid
To fold the earth in robes of shade,

From out the woods
across the mead,
The Brownies gath-
ered as agreed,
To venture boldly
and procure

The skates that would their fun insure.
As mice can get to cake and cheese
Without a key whene'er they please,
So, cunning Brownies can proceed
And help themselves to what they need.

For bolts and bars they little care
If but a nail is wanting there!
Or, failing this, with ease descend
Like Santa Claus and gain their end.
As children to the windows fly
At news of Jumbo passing by,
So rushed the eager band away
To fields of ice without delay.

17

Though far too large at heel and toe,
The skates were somehow made to go.
But out behind and out before,
Like spurs, they stuck a span or more,
Alike afflicting foe and friend

In bringing journeys to an end.
They had their slips and sudden spreads,
Where heels flew higher than their heads,
As people do, however nice,
When venturing first upon the ice.
But soon they learned to curve and wheel
And cut fine scrolls with scoring steel,
To race in clusters to and fro,
To jump and turn and backward go,
Until a rest on bed so cool,
Was more the wonder than the rule.

But from the lake they all withdrew
Some hours before the night was through,
And hastened back with lively feet
Through narrow lane and silent street,
Until they reached the broker's door
With every skate that left the store.

And, ere the first   faint gleam of day,
The skates were   safely stowed away;
Of their brief ab-   sence not a trace
Was left within the   dusty place.

THE BROWNIES ON BICYCLES.

NE evening Brownies, peeping down
    From bluffs that overlooked the town,
    Saw wheelmen passing to and fro
    Upon the boulevard below.
"It seems," said one,
    "an easy trick,
The wheel goes 'round so
    smooth and quick;
You simply sit and work
    your feet
And glide with grace along
    the street.

The pleasure would be fine indeed
If *we* could thus in line proceed."

"Last night," another answer made,
"As by the river's bank I strayed,
  Where here and there a building stands,
  And town and country-side join hands,
  Before me stood a massive wall
  With engine-rooms and chimneys tall.

"To scale the place a way I found,
  And, creeping in, looked all around;

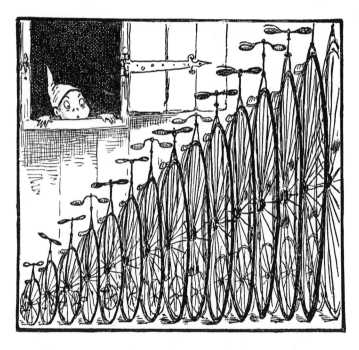

There bicycles of every grade
Are manufactured for the trade;
Some made for baby hands to guide,
And some for older folk to ride.

"Though built to keep intruders out,
   With shutters thick and casings stout,
   I noticed twenty ways or more,
   By roof, by window, wall and door,
   Where we, by exercising skill,
   May travel in and out at will."

Another spoke, in nowise slow
To catch at pleasures as they go,
         And said, "Why let another day
         Come creeping in to drag away?
                  Let's active measures now employ
                  To seize at once the promised joy.
            On bicycles quick let us ride,
            While yet our wants may be supplied."

So when the town grew hushed and still,
The Brownies ventured down the hill,
      And soon the band was
            drawing   nigh
      The building with
            the chim-
               neys
      high.

                  When people
                     lock   their   doors
                  at night,
               And double-bolt them left and right,
               And think through patents, new and old,
         To leave the burglars in the cold,

The cunning Brownies smile to see
The springing bolt and turning key;
For well they know if fancy leads
Their band to venture daring
  deeds,
The miser's gold, the mer-
  chant's ware
To them is open as the air.

Not long could door or windows stand
Fast locked before the Brownie band;
And soon the bicycles they sought
From every room and bench were brought.

The rogues ere long began to show
As many colors as the bow;
For paint and varnish lately spread
Besmeared them all from foot to head.
Some turned to jay-birds in a minute,
And some as quick might shame the linnet;
While more with crimson-tinted breast
Seemed fitted for the robin's nest.

But whether red or green or blue,
The work on hand was hurried through;
They took the wheels from blacksmith fires,
Though wanting bolts and even tires,
And rigged the parts with skill and speed
To answer well their pressing need.
And soon, enough were made complete
To give the greater part a seat,
And let the rest through cunning find
Some way of hanging on behind.
And then no spurt along the road,
Or 'round the yard their courage showed,
But twenty times a measured mile
They whirled away in single file,
Or bunched together in a crowd
If width of road or skill allowed.
At times, while rolling down the grade,
Collisions some confusion made,
For every member of the band,
At steering wished to try his hand;
Though some, perhaps, were not designed
For labor of that special kind.

But Brownies are the folk to bear
Misfortunes with unruffled air;
So on through rough and smooth they spun
Until the turning-point was won.
Then back they wheeled with every spoke,
An hour before the thrush awoke.

THE BROWNIES AT LAWN-TENNIS.

ONE evening as the woods grew dark,
    The Brownies wandered through a park,
And soon a building, quaint and small,
Appeared to draw the gaze of all.
Said one : " This place contains, no doubt,
The tools of workmen hereabout."
Another said : "You 're quite astray,
The workmen's tools are miles away ;
Within this building may be found
The fixtures for the tennis ground.
A meadow near, both long and wide,
For half the year is set aside,
And marked with many a square and court,
For those who love the royal sport.
On afternoons assembled there,
The active men and maidens fair
Keep up the game until the day
Has faded into evening gray."
"In other lands than those we tread,
    I played the game," another said,
"And proved my skill and muscle stout,
    As ' server ' and as ' striker-out.'

The lock that hangs before us there
Bears witness to the keeper's care,
And tramps or burglars might go by,
If such a sign should meet the eye.
But we, who laugh at
    locks or law
Designed to keep man-
    kind in awe,
May praise the keeper's
    cautious mind,
But all the same an en-
    trance find."

Ere long, the path that lay between
The building and the meadow green,
Was crowded with the bustling throng,
All bearing implements along;
Some lugging stakes or racket sets,
And others buried up in nets.
To set the posts and mark the ground
The proper size and shape around,

With service-line and line of base,
And courts, both left and right, in place,
Was work that caused but slight delay;
And soon the sport was under way.
And then a strange and stirring scene
Was pictured out upon the green.

Some watched the game and noted well
Where this or that one would excel.

And shouts and calls that filled the air
Proved even-handed playing there.
With anxious looks some kept the score,
And shouted "'vantage!" "game all!" or
To some, "love, forty!"—"deuce!" to more.
But when "deuce set!" the scorer cried,
Applause would ring on every side.
At times so hot the contest grew,
Established laws aside they threw,
And in the game where four should stand,
At least a dozen took a hand.
Some tangled in the netting lay
And some from base-lines strayed away.
Some hit the ball when out of place
Or scrambled through unlawful space.
But still no game was forced to halt
Because of this or greater fault.

And there they sported on the lawn
Until the ruddy streaks of dawn
Gave warning that the day was near,
And Brownies all must disappear.

THE BROWNIES' GOOD WORK.

ONE time, while Brownies passed around
An honest farmer's piece of ground,
They paused to view the garden fair
And fields of grain that needed care.
"My friends," said one who often spoke
About the ways of human folk,
"Now here's a case in point, I claim,
Where neighbors scarce deserve the name:
This farmer on his back is laid
With broken ribs and shoulder-blade,
Received, I hear, some weeks ago;
While at the village here below,
He checked a
running team,
to save
Some children
from an early
grave.
Now overripe
his harvest
stands
In waiting for
the reaper's
hands;
The piece of
wheat we
lately passed
Is shelling out
at every blast;

30

Those pumpkins in that corner plot
Begin to show the signs of rot;
The mold has fastened on their skin,
The ripest ones are caving in,
And soon the pig in yonder sty
With scornful grunt would pass
　　them by.
His Early Rose potatoes there
Are much in need of light and air;
The turnip withers where it lies,
The beet and carrot want to rise.
'Oh, pull us up!' they seem to cry
To every one that passes by;
'The frost will finish our repose,
　　The grubs are working at our toes;

Unless you come and save us soon,
We'll not be worth a picayune!'
The corn is breaking from the stalk,
The hens around the hill can walk,
And with their ever ready bill
May pick the ker- nels at their will.
His neighbors are a sordid crowd,
Who 've such a shameful waste allowed;
So wrapped in self some men can be,
Beyond their purse they seldom see;
'T is left for us to play the friend
And here a helping hand extend.
But as the wakeful chanticleer
Is crowing in the stable near,
Too little of the present night
Is left to set the matter right.

" To-morrow eve, at that dark hour
When birds grow still in leafy bower
And bats forsake the ruined pile
To exercise their wings awhile,
In yonder shady grove we 'll meet,
With all our active force complete,
Prepared to give this farmer aid
With basket, barrel, hook, and spade.

But, ere we part, one caution more:
Let some invade a druggist's store,
And bring along a coated pill;

We 'll dose the dog to keep him still.
For barking dogs, however kind,
Can oft disturb a Brownie's mind."
—When next the bat of evening flew,
And drowsy things of day withdrew,
When beetles droned across the lea,
And turkeys sought the safest tree
To form aloft a social row
And criticise the fox below,—
Then cunning Brownies might be seen
Advancing from the forest green;
Now jumping fences, as they ran,
Now crawling through (a safer plan);
Now keeping to the roads awhile,
Now "cutting corners," country style;
Some bearing hoes, and baskets more,
Some pushing barrows on before,
While others, swinging sickles bright,
Seemed eager for the grain in sight.
But in advance of all the throng
Three daring Brownies moved along,
Whose duty was to venture close
And give the barking dog his dose.

33

Now soon the work was under way,
Each chose the part he was to play:
While some who handled hoes the best
Brought "Early Roses" from their nest,
To turnip-tops some laid their hands,
More plied the hook, or twisted bands.
And soon the sheaves lay piled around,
Like heroes on disputed ground.
Now let the eye turn where it might,
A pleasing prospect was in sight;
For garden ground or larger field
Alike a busy crowd revealed:
Some pulling carrots from their bed,
Some bearing burdens on their head,
Or working at a fever heat
While prying out a monster beet.
Now here two heavy loads have met,
And there a barrow has upset,
While workers every effort strain
The rolling pumpkins to regain;

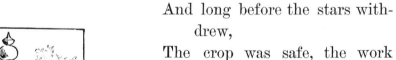

And long before the stars withdrew,
The crop was safe, the work was through.
In shocks the corn, secure and good,
Now like a Sioux encampment stood;
The wheat was safely stowed away;
In bins the "Early Roses" lay,

While carrots, tur-
nips, beets, and all
Received attention,
great and small.
When morning dawn-
ed, no sight or sound
Of friendly Brownies
could be found;
And when at last old
Towser broke
The spell, and from
his slumber woke,
He rushed around, be-
lieving still
Some mischief lay be-
hind the pill.
But though the fields
looked bare and
strange,
His mind could hardly
grasp the change.
And when the farmer
learned at morn
That safe from harm were wheat and corn,
That all his barley, oats, and rye
Were in the barn, secure and dry,
That carrots, beets, and turnips round
Were safely taken from the ground,
The honest farmer thought, of course,
His neighbors had turned out in force
While helpless on the bed he lay,
And kindly stowed his crop away.

35

But when he thanked them for their aid,
And hoped they yet might be repaid
For acting such a friendly part,
His words appeared to pierce each heart;
For well they knew that other hands
Than theirs had laid his grain in bands,
That other backs had bent in toil
To save the products of the soil.
And then they felt as such folk will
Who fail to nobly act, until
More earnest helpers, stepping in,
Do all the praise and honor win.

THE BROWNIES AT THE GYMNASIUM.

THE Brownies once, while roaming 'round,
By chance approached a college ground;
And, as they skirmished every side,
A large gymnasium they espied.
Their eyes grew bright as they surveyed
The means for exercise displayed.
The club, the weight, the hanging ring,
The horizontal bar, and swing,

The boxing-gloves that please the heart
Of him who loves the manly art,
All brought expres- sions of delight,
As one by one they came in sight.
The time was short, and words were few
That named the work for each to do.

Their mystic art, as may be found
On pages now in volumes bound,
Was quite enough to bear them in
Through walls of wood and roofs of tin.
No hasp can hold, no bolt can
    stand
Before the Brownie's tiny hand;
The sash will rise, the panel yield,
And leave him master of the
    field.—
When safe they stood
    within the hall,
A pleasant time was
    promised all.

37

Said one: "The clubs let me obtain
That Indians use upon the plain,
And here I 'll stand to test my power,
And swing them 'round my head an hour;
Though not the largest in the band,
I claim to own no infant hand;
And muscle in this arm you 'll meet
That well might grace a trained athlete.

Two goats once blocked a mountain pass,
Contending o'er a tuft of grass.
Important messages of state
Forbade me there to stand and wait;
Without a pause, the pair I neared
And seized the larger by the beard;
I dragged him from his panting foe
And hurled him to the plain below."

"For clubs," a second an-
    swered there,
"Or heavy weights I little care;
  Let those by generous nat-
    ure planned
  At heavy lifting try their
    hand;
  But give me bar or give me
    ring,
  Where I can turn, contort,
    and swing,
  And I 'll outdo, with move-
    ments fine,
  The monkey on his tropic
    vine."

Thus skill and strength and wind they tried
By means they found on every side.
Some claimed at once the high trapeze,
And there performed with grace and ease;
They turned and tumbled left and right,
As though they held existence light.
At times a finger-tip was all
Between them and a fearful fall.
On strength of toes they now depend,
Or now on coat-tails of a friend—
And had that cloth been less than best
That looms could furnish, east or west,
Some members of the Brownie race
Might now be missing from their place.

39

But fear, we know, scarce ever finds
A home within their active minds.
And little danger they could see
In what would trouble you or me.
Some stood to prove their muscle strong,
And swung the clubs both large and long
That men who met to practice there
Had often found no light affair.

A rope   they found as
'round   they ran,
And   then a "tug-of-war"
                  began;
                  First over benches, stools,
                  and chairs,
                  Then up and down the wind-
                  ing stairs,
                  They pulled and hauled and tugged
                  around,
Now giving up, now gaining ground,
Some lost their footing at the go,
And on their backs slid to and fro
Without a chance their state to mend
Until the contest found an end.

Their coats from tail to collar rent
Showed some through trying treatment went,
And more, with usage much the same,
All twisted out of shape, and lame,
Had scarce a button to their name.

The judge selected for the case
Ran here and there about the place
With warning cries and gesture wide,
And seemed unable to decide.

And there they might be tug-
ging still,
With equal strength and equal
will—
But while they struggled, stars
withdrew
And hints of morning broader
grew,
Till arrows from the rising sun
Soon made them drop the rope
and run.

PALMER COX

THE BROWNIES' FEAST.

N best of spirits, blithe and free,—
As Brownies always seem to be,—
A jovial band, with hop and leap,
Were passing through a forest deep,
When in an open space they spied
A heavy caldron, large and wide,
Where woodmen, working at their trade,
A rustic boiling-place had made.
"My friends," said one, "a chance like this
No cunning Brownie band should miss;
All unobserved, we may prepare
And boil a pudding nicely there;
Some dying embers smolder still
Which we may soon revive at will;
And by the roots of yonder tree
A brook goes babbling to the sea.
At Parker's mill, some miles below,
They 're grinding flour as white as snow;
An easy task for us to bear
Enough to serve our need from there:

42

I noticed, as I passed to-night,
A window with a broken light,
And through the opening we 'll pour
Though bolts and bars be on the door."
" And I," another Brownie cried,
" Will find the plums and currants dried;
I 'll have some here in half an hour
To sprinkle thickly through the flour;
So stir yourselves, and bear in mind
That some must spice and sugar find."
" I know," cried one," where hens have made
Their nest beneath the burdock shade —
I saw them stealing out with care
To lay their eggs in secret there.
The farmer's wife, through sun and rain,
Has sought to find that nest in vain:
They cackle by the wall of stones,
The hollow stump and pile of bones,

And by the ditch that lies below,
Where yellow weeds and nettles grow;
And draw her after everywhere
Until she quits them in despair.
The task be mine to thither lead
A band of comrades now with speed,
To help me bear a tender load
Along the rough and rugged road."
Away, away, on every side,
At once the lively Brownies glide;
Some after plums, more 'round the hill—
The shortest way to reach the mill —
While some on wings and some on legs
Go darting off to find the eggs.

A few remained upon the spot
To build a fire beneath the pot;
Some gathered bark from trunks of trees,
While others, on their hands and knees,
Around the embers puffed and blew
Until the sparks to blazes grew;
And scarcely was the kindling burned
Before the absent ones returned.
All loaded down they came, in groups,
In couples, singly, and in troops.

Upon their shoulders, heads, and backs
They bore along the floury sacks;
With plums and currants others came,
Each bag and basket filled the same;

While those who gave the hens a call
Had taken nest-egg, nest, and all;
And more, a pressing want to meet,
From some one's line had hauled a sheet,
The monstrous pudding to infold
While in the boiling pot it rolled.
The rogues were flour from head to feet
Before the mixture was complete.
Like snow-birds in a drift of snow
They worked and elbowed in the dough,
Till every particle they brought
Was in the mass before them wrought.
And soon the sheet around the pile
Was wrapped in most artistic style.
Then every plan and scheme was tried
To hoist it o'er the caldron's side.
At times, it seemed about to fall,
And overwhelm or bury all;
Yet none forsook their post through fear,
But harder worked with danger near.
They pulled and hauled and orders gave,
And pushed and pried with
   stick and stave,

Until, in spite of height and heat,
They had performed the trying feat.
To take the pudding from the pot
They might have found as hard and hot.
But water on the fire they threw,
And then to work again they flew.
And soon the steaming treasure sat
Upon a stone both broad and flat,
Which answered for a table grand,
When nothing better was at hand.

Some think that Brownies never eat,
But live on odors soft and sweet,
That through the verdant woods proceed
Or steal across the dewy mead;
But those who could have gained a sight
Of them, around their pudding white,
Would have perceived that elves of air
Can relish more substantial fare.

They clustered close, and delved and ate
Without a knife, a spoon, or plate;
Some picking out the plums with care,
And leaving all the pastry there.
While some let plums and currants go,
But paid attention to the dough.
The purpose of each Brownie's mind
Was not to leave a crumb behind,
That, when the morning sun should shine
Through leafy tree and clinging vine,

No traces of their sumptuous feast

It   might   reveal   to   man or beast;
And well they gauged   what all could bear,
When   they   their   pudding did prepare;
For when the rich   repast was done,
The   rogues   could   neither fly nor run.
—The   miller   never   missed his flour,
For Brownies wield a   mystic power;

Whate'er they take they can restore
In greater plenty than before.

THE BROWNIES  TOBOGGANING.

One evening, when the snow lay white
On level plain and mountain height,
The
Brownies
mustered, one
and all,
In answer to a spe-
cial call.

All clustered in a ring they stood
Within the shelter of the wood,
While earnest faces brighter grew
At thought of enterprises new.
Said one, " It seems that all the rage,
With human kind of every age,
Is on toboggans swift to slide
Down steepest hill or mountain side.
Our plans at once we must prepare,
And try, ourselves, that pleasure rare.
We might enough toboggans find
In town, perhaps, of every kind,
If some one chanced to know where they
Awaiting sale are stowed away."

Another spoke: " Within us lies
The power to make our own supplies;
We 'll not depend on other hands
To satisfy these new demands;
The merchants' wares we 'll let alone
And make toboggans of our own;
A lumber-yard some miles from here
Holds seasoned lumber all the year.
There pine and cedar may be found,
And oak and ash are piled around.
Some boards are thick and some are
  thin,
But all will bend like sheets of tin.
At once we 'll hasten to the spot,
And, though a fence surrounds the lot,
We 'll skirmish 'round and persevere,
And gain an entrance,— never fear."

This brought a smile to every face,
For Brownies love to climb and race,
And undertake such work as will
Bring into play their wondrous skill.
The pointers on the dial plate
Could hardly mark a later date,
Before they scampered o'er the miles
That brought them to the lumber piles,
And then they clambered, crept, and squeezed,
And gained admittance where they pleased;
For other ways than builders show
To scale a wall the Brownies know.

Some sought for birch, and some for pine,
And some for cedar, soft and fine.
With free selection well content
Soon under heavy loads they bent.
It chanced to be a windy
   night,
Which made their
   labor far from
   light;
But, though a heavy
   tax was laid
On strength and
   patience, undis-
   mayed
They worked their
   way by hook or
   crook,
And reached at last
   a sheltered nook;

PALMER COX

50

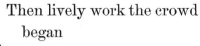

Then lively work the crowd
    began
To make toboggans true to
    plan.
The force was large, the rogues had skill,
And hands were willing — better still;
So here a twist, and there a bend,
Soon brought their labors to an end.

Without the aid of steam or glue,
They curved them like a war
    canoe;
No little forethought some dis-
    played,
But wisely "double-enders"
    made,
That should they turn, as turn
    they might,
They 'd keep the downward
    course aright;
They fashioned some for three
    or four,
And some to carry eight or more,

While some were made to take a crowd
And room for half the band allowed.
Before the middle watch of night,
The Brownies sought the mountain height,
And down the steepest grade it showed
The band in wild procession rode;
Some lay at length, some found a seat;
Some bravely stood on bracing feet.
But trouble, as you understand,
Oft moves with pleasure, hand in hand,

51

And even Brownies were not free
From evil snag or stubborn tree
That split toboggans like a quill,
And scattered riders down the hill.

With pitch and toss and plunge they flew,—
Some skimmed the drifts, some tunneled through;
Then out across the frozen plain
At dizzy speed they shot amain,

Through splintered rails and
flying gates
Of half a dozen large estates;
Until it seemed that ocean wide
Alone
c o u l d
check the
fearful ride.
Some, growing
dizzy with the speed,
At times a friendly hand would need
To help them keep their proper grip
Through all the dangers of the trip.

And thus until the stars had waned,
The sport of coasting was maintained.
Then, while they sought with lively race
In deeper woods a hiding-place,
"How strange," said one, "we never tried
Till now the wild toboggan ride!
But since we 've proved the pleasure
fine
That 's found upon the steep incline,
We 'll often muster on the height,
And make the most of every night,
Until the rains of spring descend
And bring such pleasures to an
end."
Another answered frank and free:
"In all such musters count on me;
For though my back is badly strained,
My elbow-joint and ankle sprained,

53

I 'll be the first upon the
　ground
As long as patch of snow
　is found,
And bravely do my part
　to steer
Toboggans on their wild
　career."

So every evening, foul
　or fair,
The jovial Brownies
　gathered there,
Till with the days of
　Spring, at last,
Came drenching shower
　and melting blast,
Which sent the mountain's
　ice and snow
To fill the rivers miles
　below.

THE BROWNIES' BALLOON.

WHILE rambling through the forest shade,
A sudden halt some Brownies made;
For spread about on bush and ground
An old balloon at rest they found,
That while upon some flying trip
Had given aeronauts the slip,
And, falling here in foliage green,
Through all the summer lay unseen.
The Brownies gathered fast to stare
Upon the monster lying there,

And when they learned the use and plan
Of valves and ropes, the rogues began
To lay their schemes and name a night
When all could take an airy flight.
"We want," said one, "no tame affair,
Like some that rise with heated air,
And hardly clear the chimney-top
Before they lose their life and drop.
The bag with gas must be supplied,
That will insure a lengthy ride;
When we set sail 't is not to fly
Above a spire and call it high.
The boat, or basket, must be strong,
Designed to take the crowd along;
For that which leaves a part behind
Would hardly suit the Brownie
    mind.
The works that serve the town of Bray
With gas are scarce two miles away.
To-morrow night we 'll come and bear,
        As best we can, this burden there;
        And when inflated, fit to rise,
        We 'll take a sail around the skies."

Next evening, as the scheme was planned,
The Brownies promptly were on hand;
For when some pleasure lies in view,
The absentees are always few.
But 't was no easy task to haul
The old balloon, car, ropes and all,
Across the rocks and fallen trees
And through the marshes to their knees.

56

But Brownies, persevering still,
Will keep their course through every ill,
And in the main, as history shows,
Succeed in aught they do propose.

So, though it cost them rather dear,
In scratches there and tumbles here,
They worked until the wondrous feat
Of transportation was complete.

Then while some busy fingers played
Around the rents that branches made,
An extra coil of rope was tied
In long festoons around the side,
That all the party, young and old,
Might find a trusty seat or hold.
And while they worked, they chatted free
About the wonders they would see.
Said one : " As smoothly as a kite,
We 'll rise above the clouds to-night,
And may the question settle soon,
About the surface of the moon."
Now all was ready for the gas,
And soon the lank and tangled mass
Began to flop about and rise,
As though impatient for the skies;
Then was there work for every hand
That could be mustered in the band,
To keep the growing monster low
Until they stood prepared to go;
To this and that they made it fast,
Round stones and stakes the rope
was cast;

But strong it grew and stronger still,
As every wrinkle seemed to fill;
And when at last it bounded clear,
And started on its wild career,
A rooted stump and garden gate,
It carried off as special freight.
Though all the Brownies went, a part
Were not in proper shape to start;
Arrangements hardly were complete,
Some wanted room and more a seat,
While some in acrobatic style
Must put their trust in toes awhile.
But Brownies are not hard to please,
And soon they rested at their ease;
Some found support, both safe and strong,
Upon the gate that went along,
By some the stump was utilized,
And furnished seats they highly prized.

Now, as they rose they ran afoul
Of screaming hawk and hooting owl,
And flitting bats that hooked their wings
At once around the ropes and strings,

As though content to there abide
And take the chances of the ride.
On passing through a heavy cloud,
One thus addressed the moistened crowd:
"Although the earth, from which we rise,
Now many miles below us lies,
To sharpest eye, strain as it may,
The moon looks just as far away."
"The earth is good enough for me!"

Another said, "with grassy lea,
And shady groves, of songsters full.—
Will some one give the valve a pull?"
And soon they all were well content,
To start upon a mild descent.

But once the gas commenced to go,
They lost the power to check the flow;
The more they tried control to gain,
The more it seemed to rush amain.
Then some began to wring their hands,
And more to volunteer commands;
While some were craning out to view
What part of earth their wreck would strew,
A marshy plain, a rocky shore,
Or ocean with its sullen roar.

60

It happened as they neared
the ground,
A rushing gale was sweep-
ing round,
That caught and carried them
with speed
Across the forest
and the mead.
Then lively catch-
ing might be
seen
At cedar tops and
branches green;
While still the
stump behind
them swung,
On this it caught,
to that it hung,
And, as an anchor,
played a part

They little thought of at the start.
At length, in spite of sweeping blast,
Some friendly branches held them fast:
And then, descending, safe and sound,
The daring Brownies reached the ground.
But in the tree-top on the hill
The old balloon is hanging still,
And saves the farmers on the plain
From placing scare-crows in their grain.

THE BROWNIES CANOEING.

S day in shades of evening sank,
The Brownies reached a river bank;
And there awhile stood gazing down
At students from a neighboring town,
Whose light canoes charmed every eye,
As one by one they floated by.
Said one, "We 'll follow as they go,
Until they gain the point below.

There stands a house, but
    lately made,
Wherein the club's effects are
    laid;
We 'll take possession after
    dark,
And in these strange affairs
    embark."

They all declared, at any cost,
A chance like this should ne'er be lost;
And keeping well the men in sight
They followed closely as they might.

The moon was climbing o'er the hill,
The owl was hooting by the mill,
When from the building on the sands
The boats were shoved with willing
    hands.

A "Shadow" model some explored,
And then well-pleased they rushed on
    board;
The open "Peterboro'," too,
Found its supporters—and a crew.
The Indian "Birch-bark" seemed too
    frail
And lacked the adjunct of a sail,
Yet of a load it did not
    fail,—
For all the boats were in
    demand;
As well those which with
    skill were planned

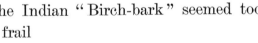

By men of keenest judgment ripe,
As those of humbler, home-made type.
And soon away sailed all the fleet
With every Brownie in his seat.

The start was promising and fine;
With little skill and less design
They steered along as suited best,
And let the current do the rest.

All nature seemed to be aware
That something strange was stirring there.
The owl to-whooed, the raven croaked;
The mink and rat with caution poked
Their heads above the wave, aghast;
While frogs a look of wonder cast
And held their breath till all had passed.
As every stream will show a bend,
If one explores from end to end,

So every river, great and small,
Must have its rapids and its fall;
And those who on its surface glide
O'er rough as well as smooth must ride.
The stream whereon had started out
The Brownie band in gleeful rout

Was wild enough to please a trout.
At times it tum- bled on its way
O'er shelving rocks and bowlders gray.
At times it formed from side to side
A brood of whirl- pools deep and wide,
That with each oth- er seemed to vie
As fated objects drifted nigh.

Ere long each watchful Brownie there,
Of all these facts grew well aware;
Some losing faith, as people will,
In their companions' care or skill,
Would seize the paddle for a time,
Until a disapproving chime
Of voices made them rest their hand,
And let still others take command.
But, spite of current, whirl, or go,
In spite of hungry tribes below,—

The eel, the craw-fish, leech, and pout,
That watched them from the starting out,
And thought each moment flitting by
Might spill them out a year's supply,—
The Brownies drifted onward still;
And though confusion baffled skill,
Canoes throughout the trying race
Kept right side up in every case.
But sport that traveled hand in hand
With horrors hardly pleased the band,
As pallid cheek and popping eye
On every side could testify;
And all agreed that wisdom lay
In steering home without delay.

So landing quick, the boats they tied
To roots or trees as chance supplied,
And plunging in the woods profound,
They soon were lost to sight and sound.

THE BROWNIES IN THE MENAGERIE

THE Brownies heard the news with
glee,
That in a city near the sea
A spacious building was designed
For holding beasts of every kind.
From polar snows, from desert
sand,
From mountain peak, and tim-
bered land,
The beasts with claw and
beasts with hoof,
All met beneath one slated
roof.
That night, like bees before
the wind,
With home in sight, and
storm behind,
The band of Brownies might
be seen,
All scudding from the forest green.
Less time it took the walls to scale
Than is required to tell the tale.
The art that makes the lock seem
weak,
The bolt to slide, the hinge to creak,
Was theirs to use as heretofore,
With good effect, on sash and door;
And soon the band stood face to face
With all the wonders of the place.

To Brownies, as to children dear,
The monkey seemed a creature queer;
They watched its skill to climb and cling,
By either toe or tail to swing;
Perhaps they got some hints that might
Come well in hand some future night,
When climbing up a wall or tree,
Or chimney, as the case might be.

Then off to other parts they'd
range
To gather 'round some creature
strange;
To watch the movements of the
bear,
Or at the spotted serpents stare.
Around the sleeping lion long
They stood an interested throng,
Debating o'er its strength of
limb,
Its heavy mane or visage grim.

The mammoth turtle from its pen
Was driven 'round and 'round again,
And though the coach proved rather
    slow
They kept it hours upon the go.
Said one, "Before your face and
    eyes
I 'll take that snake from where it
    lies,
And like a Hindoo of the East,
Benumb and charm the crawling
    beast,
Then twist him 'round me on the
    spot
And tie him in a sailor's knot."
Another then was quick to shout,
"We 'll leave that snake performance out!
I grant you all the power you claim
To charm, to tie, to twist and tame;
But let me still suggest you try
Your art when no one else is nigh.
Of all the beasts that creep or crawl
From Rupert's Land to China's wall,
In torrid, mild, or frigid zone,
The snake is best to let alone."

Against this counsel, seeming good,
At least a score of others stood.
Said one, " My friend, suppress alarm;
There 's nothing here to threaten harm.
Be sure the power that mortals hold
Is not denied the Brownies bold."

So, harmlessly as silken bands
The snakes were twisted in their hands.
Some hauled them freely 'round the place;
Some braided others in a trace;
And every knot to sailors known,
Was quickly tied, and quickly shown.

Thus, 'round from cage to cage they went,
For some to smile, and some comment
On Nature's way of dealing out
To this a tail, to that a snout

Of extra length, and then deny
To something else a fair supply.
— But when the bear and tiger growled,
And wolf and lynx in chorus howled,
And starting from its broken sleep,
The lion rose with sudden leap,
And, bounding 'round the rocking cage,
With lifted mane, roared loud with rage,
And thrust its paws between the bars,
Until it seemed to shake the stars,—

A panic seized the Brownies all,
And out they scampered from the hall,
As if they feared incautious men
Had built too frail a prison pen.

72

THE BROWNIES' CIRCUS.

ONE night the circus was in town
With tumbling men and painted clown,
And Brownies came from forest deep
Around the tent to climb and creep,
And through the canvas, as they might
Of inner movements gain a sight.

73

Said one, "A chance we'll hardly find
That better suits the Brownie mind;
To-night when all this great array
Of people take their homeward way,
We'll promptly make a swift descent
And take possession of the tent,
And here, till morning light is shown,
We'll have a circus of own."

"I best," cried one, "of all the band
The elephant can take in hand;
I noticed how they led him round
And marked the place he may be found;
On me you may depend to keep
The monster harmless as a sheep."

The laughing crowd that filled the place,
Had hardly homeward turned its face,
Before the eager waiting band
Took full possession as they planned,
And 'round they scampered left and
   right

To see what offered most delight.
Cried one, "If I can only find
The whip, I'll have a happy mind;
     For I'll be master of the ring
     And keep the horses on the spring,
     Announce the names of those who ride,
     And snap the whip on every side."
Another said, "I'll be a clown;
I saw the way they tumble down,
And how the cunning rogues contrive
To always keep the fun alive."

With such remarks away they went
At this or that around the tent;
The wire that not an hour before
The Japanese had traveled o'er
From end to end with careful stride,
Was hunted up and quickly tried.
Not one alone upon it stepped,
But up by twos and threes they crept,
Until the strand appeared to bear
No less than half the Brownies there.
Some showed an easy, graceful pose,
But some put little faith in toes,
And thought that fingers, after all,
Are best if one begins to fall.

When weary of a sport they grew,
Away to other tricks they flew.
They rode upon the rolling ball
Without regard to slip or fall;
Both up and down the steep incline
They kept their place, with balance fine,
Until it bounded from the road,
And whirled away without its load.

75

They galloped 'round the dusty ring
Without a saddle, strap or string,
And jumped through hoops both large and small,
And over banners, poles and all.

In time the elephant was found
And held as though in fetters bound;
Their mystic power controlled the beast,—
He seemed afraid to move the least,
But filled with wonder, limp and lax,
He stood and trembled in his tracks,
While all the band from first to last
Across his back in order passed.

So thus they saw the moments fly
Till dawn began to paint the sky;
And then by every flap and tear
They made their way to open air,
And off through lanes and alleys passed
To reach their hiding-place at last.

77

THE BROWNIES AT BASE-BALL.

NE evening, from a shaded spot,
The Brownies viewed a level lot

Where clubs from different cities came
To play the nation's favorite game.

Then spoke a member of the band:

"This game extends throughout the land;
No city, town, or village 'round,
But has its club, and diamond ground,
With bases marked, and paths between,
And seats for crowds to view the scene.
At other games we've not been slow
Our mystic art and skill to show;
Let's take our turn at ball and bat,
And prove ourselves expert at that."

Another answered: "I 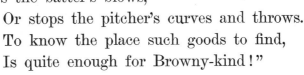 have planned
A method to equip   our band.

There is a firm in yonder town,
Whose goods have won them wide renown;
Their special branch of business lies
In sending forth these club supplies.
The balls are wound as hard as stones,
The bats are turned as smooth as bones,
And masks are made to guard the nose
Of him who fears the batter's blows,

Or stops the pitcher's curves and throws.
To know the place such goods to find,
Is quite enough for Browny-kind!"

When hungry bats came forth to wheel
'Round eaves and find their evening meal,
The cunning Brownies sought the store,
To work their way through sash and door.
And soon their beaming faces told
Success had crowned their efforts
    bold.
A goodly number of the throng
Took extra implements along,

In case of mishap on the way,
Or loss, or breakage during play.
The night was clear, the road was good,
And soon within the field they stood.

Then games were played without a pause,
According to the printed laws.
There, turn about, each took
  his place
At first or third or second
  base,

PALMER COX,

At left or right or center field,
To pitch, to catch, or bat to wield,
Or else as "short-stop" standing by
To catch a "grounder" or a "fly."

Soon every corner of the ground
Its separate set of players found.
A dozen games upon the green,
With ins and outs might there be seen;
The umpires noting all with care
To tell if hits were foul or fair,

The "strikes" and "balls" to plainly shout,
And say if men were "safe" or "out,"
And give decision just and wise
When knotty questions would arise.

But many Brownies thought it best
To leave the sport and watch the rest;
And from the seats or fences high
They viewed the scene with anxious eye
And never failed, the contest through,
To render praise when praise was due.

While others, freed from games on hand,
In merry groups aside would stand,
And pitch and catch with rarest skill
To keep themselves in practice still.

Now "double plays" and balls well curved
And "base hits" often were observed,
While "errors" were but seldom seen
Through all the games upon that green.

Before the flush of morn arose
To bring their contests to a close,
The balls and bats in every case
Were carried back and put in place;
And when the Brownies left the store,
All was in order as before.

THE BROWNIES AND THE BEES.

WHILE Brownies once were rambling through
A forest where tall timber grew,
The hum of bees above their head
To much remark and wonder led.
They gazed at branches in the air
And listened at the roots with care,
And soon a pine of giant size
Was found to hold the hidden prize.
Said one : " Some wild bees here have made
Their home within the forest shade,
Where neither fox nor prying bear
Can steal the treasure gathered there."
Another spoke: "You 're quick and bright,
And as a rule judge matters right;
But here, my friend, you 're all astray,
And like the blind mole grope your way.
I chance well to remember still,
How months ago, when up the hill,

83

A farmer near, with bell and horn,
Pursued a swarm one sunny morn.
The fearful din the town awoke,
The clapper from his bell he
   broke;
But still their queen's directing cry

The bees heard o'er the clamor high;
And held their bearing for this pine
As straight as runs the country line.
With taxes here, and failures there,
The man can ill such losses bear.
In view of this, our duty's clear:
To-morrow night we'll muster here,
And when we give this tree a fall,
In proper shape we'll hive them all,

And take the queen and working throng
And lazy drones where they belong."

Next evening, at the time they 'd set,
Around the pine the Brownies met
With tools collected, as they sped
From mill and shop and farmer's shed;
While some, to all their wants alive,
With ready hands procured a hive.

Ere work began, said one: " I fear
But little sport awaits us here.
Be sure a trying task we 'll find;
The bee is fuss and fire combined.
Let 's take him in his drowsy hour,
Or when palavering to the flower.
For bees, however wild or tame,
In all lands are about the same;
And those will rue it who neglect
To treat the buzzer with respect."

Ere long, by steady grasp and blow,
The towering tree was leveled low;
And then the hive was made to rest
In proper style above the nest,
Until the queen and all her train
Did full and fair possession gain.

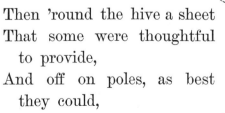Then 'round the hive a sheet  was tied,
That some were thoughtful
   to provide,
And off on poles, as best
   they could,
They bore the burden from the wood.

But trouble, as one may divine,
Occurred at points along the line.

'T was bad enough on level ground,
Where, now and then, *one* exit found;

But when the Brownies lacked a road,
Or climbed the fences with their load,—
Then numbers of the prisoners there
Came trooping out to take the air,

And managed straight enough to fly
To keep excitement running high.

With branches broken off to suit,
And grass uplifted by the root,

In vain some daring Brownies tried
To brush the buzzing plagues aside.
Said one, whose features proved to all
That bees had paid his face a call:
"I 'd rather dare the raging main
Than meddle with such things again."
"The noble voice," another cried,
"Of duty still must rule and guide,—
Or in the ditch the sun would see
The tumbled hive for all of me."

And when at last the fence they found
That girt the farmer's orchard 'round,
And laid the hive upon the stand,
There hardly was, in all the band,
A single Brownie who was free
From some reminders of the bee.

But thoughts of what a great surprise
Ere long would light the farmer's eyes
Soon drove away from every brain
The slightest thought of toil or pain.

THE BROWNIES ON ROLLER SKATES.

THE Brownies planned at close of day
    To reach a town some miles away,
    Where roller skating, so 't was said,
    Of all amusements kept ahead.
Said one: " When deeper shadows fall,
    We 'll cross the river, find the hall,

And learn the nature of the sport
Of which we hear such good report."

To reach the bridge that led to town,
With eager steps they hastened down;
But recent rains had caused a rise —
The stream was now a fearful size;
The bridge was nearly swept away,
Submerged in parts, and wet with spray.

But when the cunning Brownies get
Their mind on some maneuver set,
Nor wind nor flood, nor frost nor fire
Can ever make the rogues retire.

Some walked the dripping logs with ease,
While others crept on hands and knees
With movements rather safe than fast,
And inch by inch the danger passed.

Now, guided by the rumbling sound
That told where skaters circled 'round,
Through dimly lighted streets they flew,
And close about the building drew.

Without delay the active band,
By spouts and other means at hand,

Of skill and daring furnished proof
And gained possession of the roof;
Then through the skylight viewed the show
Presented by the crowds below.

Said one: "While I survey that floor
I 'm filled with longing more and more,

And discontent with me will bide
Till 'round the rink I smoothly glide.
At night I 've ridden through the air,
Where bats abide, and owls repair;
I 've rolled in surf of ocean wide,
And coasted down the mountain-side;
And now to sweep around a hall
On roller skates would crown it all."

" My plans," the leader answer made,
" Are in my mind already laid.
Within an hour the folk below
Will quit their sport and homeward go;
Then will the time   be ripe, indeed,
For us to leave this   roof with speed,
And prove how well   our toes and heels
We may command   when set on wheels."

When came the   closing hour at last,
And people from   the rink had passed,
The Brownies hurried down to find
The roller skates they 'd left behind.

Then such a scene was there as few
May ever have a chance to view.
Some hardly circled 'round the place,
Before they moved with ease and grace,
And skated freely to and fro,
Upon a single heel or toe.
Some coats were torn beyond repair,
By catches here and clutches there,
When those who felt their faith give way,
Groped right and left without delay;

While some who strove their friends to aid,
Upon the floor themselves were laid,
To spread confusion there awhile,
As large and larger grew the pile.

Some rose with fingers out of joint,
Or black and blue at every point;

And few but felt some portion sore,
From introductions to the floor.
But such mishaps were lost to sight,
Amid the common wild delight,—
For little plaint do Brownies make
O'er bump or bruise or even break.

But stars at length began to wane,
And dawn came creeping through the pane;
And much against the will of all,
The rogues were forced to leave the hall.

THE BROWNIES AT THE SEASIDE.

WITHIN a forest dark
and wide,
Some distance from the
ocean side,
A band of Brownies played around
On mossy stone or grassy mound,
Or, climbing through the branch-
ing tree,
Performed their antics wild and
free.

When one, arising in his place
With sparkling eyes and beaming face
Soon won attention from the rest,
And thus the listening throng addressed:
" For years and years, through heat and cold,
Our home has been this forest old;
The saplings which we used to bend
Now like a schooner's masts ascend.

Yet here we live, content to ride
A springing bough with childish
    pride,
Content to bathe in brook or bog
Along with lizard, leech, and
    frog;
We 're far behind the age you 'll
    find
If once you note the human kind.

The modern youths no longer lave
Their limbs beneath the muddy wave
Of meadow pool or village pond,
But seek the ocean far beyond.
　　If pleasure in the sea is found
　　Not offered by the streams around,
　　The Brownie band at once should haste
　　　　These unfamiliar joys to taste;
　　　　No torch nor lantern's ray
　　　　we 'll need
　　　　　　To show our path o'er
　　　　　　dewy mead,
　　　　　　The ponds and pit-
　　　　　　falls in the swale,
　　　　　　The open ditch,
　　　　　　the slivered rail,
　　　　　　The poison vine
　　　　　　and thistle high
　　　　　　Show clear be-
　　　　　　fore the Brown-
　　　　　　ie's eye."
　　　　　—Next evening, as
　　　　　their plan they 'd laid,
　　　　The band soon gathered
in the shade.
　　　　All clustered like a swarm of bees
They darted from the sheltering trees;
And straight across the country wide
Began their journey to the tide.
And when they neared the beach at last,—
The stout, the lean, the slow, the fast,—
'T was hard to say, of all the lot,
Who foremost reached the famous spot.

"And now," said one with active mind,
"What proper garments can we find?
  In bathing costume, as you know,
  The people in the ocean go."

Another spoke, "For such demands,
The building large that yonder stands,

As one can see on passing by,
Is full of garments clean and dry.
There every fashion, loose or tight,
We may secure with labor light."

Though Brownies never carry keys,
They find an entrance where they please;

And never do they chuckle more
Than when some miser bars his door;
For well they know that, spite of locks,
Of rings and staples, bolts and blocks,
Were they inclined to play such prank
He 'd find at morn an empty bank.
So now the crafty Brownie crew
Soon brought the bathing-suits to view;
Some, working on the inner side,
The waiting throng without sup-
   plied.—

'T was busy work, as may be guessed,
Before the band was fully dressed;
Some still had cloth enough to lend,
Though shortened up at either end;
Some ran about to find a pin,
While others rolled, and puckered in,

And made the best of what they found,
However strange it hung around.

Then, when a boat was manned with care
To watch for daring swimmers there,—

Lest some should venture, over-bold,
And fall a prey to cramp and cold,—
A few began from piers to leap
And plunge at once in water deep,
But more to shiver, shrink, and shout
As step by step they ventured out;
While others were content to stay
In shallow surf, to duck and play
Along the lines that people laid
To give the weak and timid aid.

It was a sight one should behold,
When o'er the crowd the breakers rolled;—
One took a header through the wave,
One floated like a chip or stave,
While others there, at every plunge,
Were taking water like a sponge.

But while the surf they tumbled through,
They reckoned moments as they flew,
And kept in mind their homeward race
Before the sun should show his face.

For sad and painful is the fate
Of those who roam abroad too late;
And well may Brownies bear in mind
The hills and vales they leave behind,
When far from native haunts they run,
As oft they do, in quest of fun.

But, ere they turned to leave the strand,
They made a vow with lifted hand
That every year, when summer's glow
Had warmed the ocean spread below,
They 'd journey far from grove and glen
To sport in rolling surf again.

THE BROWNIES AND THE
SPINNING-WHEEL.

ONE evening, with the falling dew,
Some Brownies 'round a cottage drew.
Said one : " I 've learned the reason why
We miss the ' Biddy, Biddy ! ' cry,
That every morning brought a score
Of fowls around this cottage door;
'T is rheumatism most severe
That keeps the widow prisoned here.
Her sheep go bleating through the field,
In quest of salt no herb can yield,
To early roost the fowls withdraw
While each bewails an empty craw,
And sore neglect you may discern
On every side, where'er you turn.
If aid come to the widow's need,
From Brownies' hands it must proceed."
Another said : " The wool, I know,
Went through the mill a month ago.

101

I saw them when they bore the sack
Up yonder hill, a wondrous pack
That caught the branches overhead,
And round their heels the gravel spread.
Her spinning-wheel is lying there
In fragments quite beyond repair.
A passing goat, with manners bold,
Mistook it for a rival old,

And knocked it 'round for half an
   hour
With all his noted butting power.
They say it was a striking scene,
That twilight conflict on the green;
The wheel was resting on the shed,
The frame around the garden spread,
Before the goat had gained his sight,
And judged the article aright."

A third remarked: "I call to mind
Another wheel that we may find,
Though somewhat worn by use and
   time,
It seems to be in order prime;
Now, night is but a babe as yet,
The dew has scarce the clover wet;
By running fast and working hard
We soon can bring it to the yard;
Then stationed here in open air
The widow's wool shall be our care."

This suited all, and soon with zeal
They started off to find the wheel;
Their course across the country lay
Where great obstructions barred the
   way;
But Brownies seldom go around
However rough or wild the ground.

O'er rocky slope and marshy bed,
With one accord they pushed ahead,—

Across the tail-race of a mill,
And through a churchyard on the hill.

They found the wheel, with head and feet,
And band and fixtures, all complete;

And soon beneath the trying load
Were struggling on the homeward road.

They had some trouble, toil, and care,
Some hoisting here, and hauling there;

At times, the wheel upon a fence
Defied them all to drag it thence,
As though determined to remain
And serve the farmer, guarding grain.
But patient head and willing hand
Can wonders work in every land;

And cunning Brownies never yield,
But aye as victors leave the field.

Some ran for sticks, and some for pries,
And more for blocks on which to rise,
That every hand or shoulder there,
In such a pinch might do its share.

Before the door they set the wheel,
And near at hand the winding reel,
That some might wind while others spun,
And thus the task be quickly done.

No time was wasted, now, to find
What best would suit each hand or mind.
Some through the cottage crept about
To find the wool and pass it out;
With some to turn, and some to pull,
And some to shout, " The spindle 's full!"
The wheel gave out a droning song,—
The work in hand was pushed along.

Their mode of action and their skill
With wonder might a spinster fill;
For out across the yard entire
They spun the yarn like endless wire,—
Beyond the well with steady haul,
Across the patch of beans and all,
Until the walls, or ditches wide,
A greater stretch of wool denied.

The widow's yarn was quickly wound
In tidy balls, quite large and round.

And ere the night began to fade,
The borrowed wheel at home was laid;
And none the worse for rack or wear,
Except a blemish here and there,
A spindle bent, a broken band,—
'T was ready for the owner's hand.

THE BROWNIES' VOYAGE.

ONE night, a restless Brownie band
    Resolved to leave their native strand,
And visit islands fair and green,
That in the distance might be seen.

In answer to a summons wide,
The Brownies came from every side—
A novel spectacle they made,
All mustered in the forest shade.
With working implements they came,
Of every fashion, use, and name.

Said one, " How many times have we
Surveyed those islands in the sea,
And longed for means to thither sail
And ramble over hill and vale !

That pleasure rare we may command,
Without the aid of human hand.
And ere the faintest streak of gray
Has advertised the coming day,
A sturdy craft, both tough and tall,
With masts and halyards, shrouds and all,
With sails to spread, and helm to guide,
Completed from the ways shall glide.
So exercise your mystic power
And make the most of every hour!"

With axes, hammers, saws, and rules,
Dividers, squares, and boring tools,
The active Brownies scattered 'round,
And every one his labor found.

Some fell to chopping
down the trees,
And some to hewing
ribs and knees;
While more the
ponderous keelson
made,
And fast the shapely
hull was laid.
Then over all they
clambered soon,
Like bees around
their hive in June.
'T was hammer, ham-
mer, here and there,
And rip and racket
everywhere,

109

While some were spiking planks and beams,
The calkers stuffed the yawning seams,
And poured the resin left and right,
To make her stanch and water-tight.
Some busily were bringing nails,
And bolts of canvas for the sails,
And coils of rope of every size
To make the ratlines, shrouds, and guys.
It mattered little whence it came,
Or who a loss of stock might claim;
Supply kept even with demand,
Convenient to the rigger's hand.

'T was marvelous to see how fast
The vessel was together cast;
Until, with all its rigs and stays,
It sat prepared to leave the ways.
It but remained to name it now,
And break a bottle on the bow,
To knock the wedges from the side,
And from the keel, and let it slide.

And when it rode upon the sea,
The Brownies thronged the deck with glee,
And veering 'round in proper style,
They bore away for nearest isle.

But those who will the ocean brave
Should be prepared for wind and wave;
For storms will rise, as many know,
When least we look for squall or blow.
And soon the sky was overcast,
And waves were running high and fast;

Then some were sick and some were filled
With fears that all their ardor chilled;
But, as when dangers do assail
The humankind, though some may quail,
There will be found a few to face
The danger, and redeem the race,—

So, some brave
Brownies nobly
stood
And manned the ship
as best they could.
Some staid on deck
to sound for bars;
Some went aloft to
watch for stars;
And some around the
rudder hung,
And here and there
the vessel swung,
While others, strung
on yard and mast,
Kept shifting sails
to suit the blast.

At times, the bow
was high in air,
And next the stern
was lifted there.

So thus it tumbled, tossed, and rolled,
And shipped enough to fill the hold,
Till more than once it seemed as though
To feed the fish they all must go.

But still they bravely tacked and veered,
And hauled, and reefed, and onward
  steered;
While screaming birds around them
  wheeled,
As if to say: "Your doom is sealed";
And hungry gar and hopeful shark
In shoals pursued the creaking bark,
Still wondering how it braved a gale
That might have made Columbus pale.

The rugged island, near them now,
Was looming on their starboard bow;
But knowing not the proper way
Of entering its sheltered bay,
They simply kept their canvas spread,
And steered the vessel straight ahead.
The birds were distanced in the race;
The gar and shark gave up the chase,
And turning back, forsook the keel,
And lost their chances of a meal.

For now the ship to ruin flew,
As though it felt its work was through,
And soon it stranded, "pitch and toss,"
Upon the rocks, a total loss.
The masts and spars went by the board—
The hull was shivered like a gourd!
But yet, on broken plank and rail,
On splintered spars and bits of sail
That strewed for miles the rugged strand,
The Brownies safely reached the land.

Now, Brownies lack the power, 't is said,
Of making twice what once they 've made;
So all their efforts were in vain
To build and launch the ship again;—
And on that island, roaming 'round,
That Brownie band for years was found.

THE BROWNIES' RETURN.

ONCE while the Brownies lay at ease
About the roots of rugged trees,
And listened to the dreary moan
Of tides around their island lone,
Said one: "My friends, unhappy here,
We spend our days from year to year.
We 're cornered in, and hardly boast
A run of twenty leagues at most.

You all remember well, I ween,
The night we reached this island green,
When flocks of fowl around us wailed,
And followed till their pinions failed.
And still our ship at every wave
To sharks a creaking promise gave,
Then spilled us out in breakers white,
To gain the land as best we might.
Since then how oft we 've tried in vain
To reach our native haunts again,
Where roaming freely, unconfined,
Would better suit our roving mind.

" To-night, while wandering by the sea,
A novel scheme occurred to me,
As I beheld in groups and rows
The weary fowl in deep repose.
They sat as motionless as though
The life had left them years ago.
The albatross and crane are there,
The loon, the gull, and gannet rare.
An easy task for us to creep
Around the fowl, while fast asleep,
And at a given signal spring
Aboard, before they spread a wing,
And trust to them to bear us o'er,
In safety to our native shore."

Another spoke : " I never yet
Have shunned a risk that others met,
But here uncommon dangers lie,
Suppose the fowl should seaward fly,

And never landing, course about,
And drop us, when their wings gave out?"

To shallow schemes that will not bring
A modest risk, let cowards cling!
The first replied. "A Brownie shows
The best where dangers thickest close.
But, hear me out: by sea and land,
Their habits well I understand.
When rising first they circle wide,
As though the strength of wings they tried,
Then steering straight across the bay,
To yonder coast a visit pay.
But granting they for once should be
Inclined to strike for open sea,
The breeze that now is rising fast,
Will freshen to a whistling blast,
And landward sweeping, stronger still,
Will drive the fowl against their will."

Now at his heels, with willing feet,
They followed to the fowls' retreat.
'T was hard to scale the rugged breast
Of crags, where birds took nightly rest.
But some on hands, and some on knees,
And more by vines or roots of trees,
From shelf to shelf untiring strained,
And soon the windy summit gained.
With bated breath, they gathered round;
They crawled with care along the ground.
By this, one paused; or that, one eyed;
Each chose the bird he wished to ride.

When all had done the best they
   could,
And waiting for the signal
   stood,
It hardly took a moment's space
For each to scramble to his
   place.

Some seized a neck and some a head,
And some a wing, and some a shred
Of tail, or aught that nearest lay,
To help them mount without delay.
Then rose wild flaps and piercing screams,
As sudden starting from their dreams
The wondering fowl in sore dismay
Brought wings and muscles into play.
Some felt the need of longer sleep,
And hardly had the strength to "cheep;"

While others seemed to find a store
Of screams they 'd never found before.
—But off like leaves or flakes of snow
Before the gale the Brownies go,
Away, away, through spray or cloud
As fancy led, or load allowed.
Some birds to poor advantage showed,
As, with an oddly balanced load,
Now right or left at random cast,

They flew, the sport
of every blast;
While fish below
had aching eyes
With gazing upward
at the prize.
They followed still
from mile to mile,
Believing fortune
yet would smile;
While plainer to the
Brownies grew
The hills and vales
that well they
knew.
"I see," said one,
who, from his
post
Between the wings,
could view the
coast,
"The lofty peaks we
used to climb

To gaze upon the
scene sublime."
A second cried:
"And there's the
bay
From which our ves-
sel bore away!"
"And I," another
cried, "can see
The shady grove,
the very tree
We met beneath
the night we
planned
To build a ship and
leave the land!"

All in confusion
now at last,
The birds upon the
shore were cast.
Some, tumbling
through thick
branches, fell

And spilled the load that clung so well.
Some, "topsy-turvy" to the ground,
Dispersed their riders all around;
And others still could barely get
To shores where land and water met.

Congratulations then began,
As here and there the Brownies ran,

To learn if all had held their grip
And kept aboard throughout the trip.
"And now," said one, " that all are o'er
In safety to our native shore,
You see, so wasted is the night,
Orion's belt is out of sight;
And ere the lamp of Venus fades
We all must reach the forest shades.

THE BROWNIES' SINGING-SCHOOL.

AS mists of evening deeper grew,
The Brownies 'round a comrade drew,
An interesting tale to hear
About a village lying near.
  " Last night," said he, " I heard arise
  From many throats discordant cries.
  At once I followed up the sound,
  And soon, to my amazement, found
  It issued from a building small
  That answered for the county hall.

"I listened there around the door,
By village time, an hour or more;
Until I learned beyond a doubt
A singing-school caused all the rout.

Some, like the hound, would keep ahead,
And others seemed to lag instead.
Some singers, struggling with the tune,
Outscreamed the frightened northern loon.
Some mocked the pinched or wheezing cry
Of locusts when the wheat is nigh,
While grumbling bassos shamed the strain
Of bull-frogs calling down the rain."

The Brownies labor heart and hand
All mysteries to understand;
And if you think those Brownies bold
Received the news so plainly told,
And thought no more about the place,
You 're not familiar with the race.

When scholars next their voices tried,
The Brownies came from every side;
With ears to knot-holes in the wall,
To door-jambs, thresholds, blinds, and all,
They listened to the jarring din
Proceeding from the room
within.

PALMER COX

Said one at length, " It seems to me
The master here will earn his fee,
If he from such a crowd can bring
A single person trained to sing."
Another said, " We 'll let them try
Their voices till their throats are dry,
And when for home they all depart,
We 'll not be slow to test our art."

That night the Brownies cheered to find
The music had been left behind;
And when they stood within the hall,
And books were handed 'round to all,
They pitched their voices, weak or strong,
At solemn verse and lighter song.

John-ny Mor-gan play'd the organ, The father beat the drum, The sis-ter play'd the tam-bou-rine,

Some sought a good old hymn to try;
Some grappled with a lullaby;
A few a painful effort made
To struggle through a serenade;
While more preferred the lively air
That, hinting less of love or care,
Possessed a chorus loud and bright
In which they all could well unite.
At times some member tried to rule,
And took control of all the school;

But soon, despairing, was content
To let them follow out their bent.

They sung both high and low, the same,
As fancy led or courage came.

Some droned the tune through teeth or nose,
Some piped like quail, or cawed like crows
That, hungry, wait the noonday horn
To call the farmer from his corn.

By turns at windows some would stay
To note the signs of coming day.
At length the morning, rising, spread
Along the coast her streaks of red,
And drove the Brownies from the place
To undertake the homeward race.

But many members of the band
Still kept their singing-books in hand,
Determined not with those to part
Till they were perfect in the art.
And oft in leafy forest shade,
In after times, a ring they made,
To pitch the tune, and raise the voice,
To sing the verses of their choice,
And scare from branches overhead
The speckled thrush and robin red,
And make them feel the time had come
When singing birds might well be dumb.

THE BROWNIES' FRIENDLY TURN.

ONE night while snow was lying deep
On level plain and mountain steep,
A sheltered nook the Brownies found,
Where conversation might go 'round.
Said one: "The people hereabout
Their wood supply have taken out;
But while they stripped the timber lot,
The village parson they forgot.

Now that good man, the story goes,
As best he can, must warm his toes."

Another spoke: "The way is clear
To show both skill and courage here.
You 're not the sort, I know, to shirk:
And coward-like to flee from work.
You act at once whene'er you find
A chance to render service kind,
Nor wait to see what others do
In matters that appeal to you.

"This task in waiting must be done
Before another day has run.
The signs of change are in the air;
A storm is near though skies are fair;
As oft when smiles the broadest lie,
The tears are nearest to the eye.
To work let every Brownie bend,
And prove to-night the parson's friend.
We 'll not take oxen from the stall,
That through the day must pull and haul,
Nor horses from the manger lead;
But let them take the rest they need.
Since mystic power is at our call,
By our own selves we 'll do it all.
Our willing arms shall take the place
Of clanking chain and leathern trace,
And 'round the door the wood we 'll strew
Until we hide the house from view."

At once the Brownies sought the ground
Where fuel could with ease be found,—
A place where forest-fires had spread,
And left the timber scorched and dead.

127

And there throughout the chilly night
They tugged and tore with all their might;
Some bearing branches as their load;
With lengthy poles still others strode,

Or struggled till they scarce could see,
With logs that bent them like a V;
While more from under drifts of snow
Removed old trees, and made them go
Like plows along the icy street,

With half their limbs and roots complete.
Some found it hard to train their log
To keep its place through jolt and jog,
While some, mistaking ditch for road,
Were almost buried with their load,
And but for friends and promptest care,
The morning light had found them there.

The wind that night was cold and keen,
And frosted Brownies oft were seen.
They clapped their hands and stamped their toes,
They rubbed with snow each numbing nose,
And drew the frost from every face
Before it proved a painful case.

And thus, in spite of every ill,
The task was carried forward still.
Some were by nature well designed
For work of this laborious kind,
And never felt so truly great,
As when half crushed beneath a weight.
While wondering comrades stood aghast,
And thought each step must be the last.

But some were slight and ill could bear
The heavy loads that proved their share,

129

Though at some sport or cunning plan
They far beyond their comrades ran.

Around the house some staid to pile
The gathered wood in proper style;
Which ever harder work they found
As high and higher rose the mound.

Above the window-sill it grew,
And next, the cornice hid from view;
And, ere the dawn had forced a stop,
The pile o'erlooked the chimney-top.

Some hands were sore, some backs were blue,
And legs were scraped with slipping through
Where ice and snow had left their mark
On rounded log and smoothest bark.

That morning, when the parson rose,
Against the pane he pressed his nose,
And tried the outer world to scan
To learn how signs of weather ran.

But, 'round the house, behind, before,
In front of window, shed, and door,
The wood was piled to such a height
But little sky was left in sight!

When next he climbed his pulpit stair,
He touched upon the strange affair,
And asked a blessing rich to fall
Upon the heads and homes of all
Who through the night had worked so hard
To heap the fuel 'round the yard.

His hearers knew they had no claim
To such a blessing if it came,
But whispered: "We don't understand—
It must have been the Brownie Band."

THE BROWNIES' FOURTH OF JULY.

WHEN Independence Day was nigh,
And children laid their pennies by,
Arranging plans how every cent
Should celebrate the grand event,
The Brownies in their earnest way
Expressed themselves about the day.
Said one: "The time is drawing near—
To every freeman's heart so dear—
When citizens throughout the land,
From Western slope to Eastern
  strand,

PALMER COX

Will celebrate with booming gun
Their liberties so dearly won!"

"A fitting time," another cried,
"For us, who many sports have tried,
    To introduce our mystic art
    And in some manner play a part."
    A third replied, with beaming face:
    "Trust me to lead you to a place
    Where fireworks of every kind
    Are made to suit the loyal mind.

"There, Roman candles are in store,
And bombs that like a cannon roar;
While 'round the room one may behold
Designs of every size and mold,—
The wheels that turn, when all ablaze,
And scatter sparks a thousand ways;
The eagle bird, with pinions spread;
The busts of statesmen ages dead;
And him who led his tattered band
Against invaders of the land
Until he shook the country free
From grasp of kings beyond the sea.

"We may, from this supply, with ease
Secure a share whene'er we please;
And on these hills behind the town
That to the plain go sloping down,
    We 'll take position, come what may,
    And celebrate the Nation's Day."

    That eve, when stars began to shine,
    The eager band was formed in line,

And, acting on the plans well laid,
A journey to the town was made.

The Brownies never go astray,
However puzzling is the way;
With guides before and guards behind,
They cut through every turn and wind,
Until a halt was made at last
Before a building bolted fast.
But those who think they 'd turn around
And leave because no keys are found
Should entertain the thought no more,
But study up the Brownie lore.

They rummaged boxes piled around
And helped themselves to what they found,
Some eager to secure the wheel
That would so many sparks reveal.
Some active members of the band
To bombs and crackers turned their hand,
While more those emblems sought to find
That call the Nation's birth to mind,
And bring from every side the shout
When all their meaning blazes out.

Ere long, upon the homeward road
They hastened with their novel load;
And when the bell in chapel tower
Gave notice of the midnight hour,

The ruddy flame, the turning wheel,
The showering sparks and deafening peal
Showed Brownies in the proper way
Gave welcome to the glorious day.

The lighted eagles, through the night,
Looked down like constellations bright;
The rockets, whizzing to and fro,
Lit up the slumbering town below;

While, towering there with eyes of fire,
As when he made his foes retire,
Above all emblems duly raised,
The Father of his Country blazed.

But ere the Brownies' large supply
Had gone to light the summer sky,
   Some plasters would have served the   band
   Much better than the goods on   hand;
   For there were cases all   about
   Where Brownies thought the   fuse was out,
   Till with a sudden fizz   and flare
   It caught the jokers   unaware.

At times, in spite of warning   cries,
Some proved too slow at clos-   ing eyes;
Some ears were stunned,   some noses got
Too close to something   quick and hot,
And fingers bore for   days and weeks
The trace of hasty   powder's freaks.

Some dodging   'round would get a share
Of splendor   meant for upper air,
And with   a black or speckled face
   They ran about from place to place,
   To find new dangers blaze and burn
   On every side where'er they 'd turn.

   But few were there who felt afraid
   Of bursting bomb or fusillade,
   And to the prize they 'd stick and hang
   Until it vanished with a "bang,"
   Or darting upward seemed to fly
   On special business to the sky.

But there, while darkness wrapped the hill,
The Brownies celebrated still;
For, pleasures such as this they found
But seldom in their roaming 'round;
And with reluctant feet they fled
When morning tinged the sky with red.

THE BROWNIES IN THE TOY-SHOP.

As SHADES of evening settled down,
The Brownies rambled through the town,
To pry at this, to pause at that;
By something else to hold a chat,
And in their free and easy vein
Express themselves in language plain.

At length before a store, their
eyes
Were fixed with wonder and
surprise
On toys of wood, and wax, and
tin,
And toys of rubber piled within.

PALMER COX

Said one, "In all our wandering 'round,
A sight like this we never found.
When such a passing glimpse we gain,
What marvels must the shelves contain!"

> Another said, "It must be here
> Old Santa Claus comes every year
> To gather up his large supply,
> When Christmas Eve is drawing nigh,
> That children through the land may find
> They still are treasured in his mind."

A third remarked, "Ere long he may
Again his yearly visit pay;
Before he comes to strip the place,
We 'll rummage shelf, and box, and case,
Until the building we explore
From attic roof to basement floor,
And prove what pleasure may be found
In all the wonders stowed around."

> Not long were they content to view
> Through dusty panes those wonders new;
> And, in a manner quite their own,
> They made their way through wood and stone.

> And then surprises met the band
> In odd conceits from every land.
> Well might the Brownies stand and stare
> At all the objects crowded there!
> Here, things of gentle nature lay
> In safety, midst the beasts of prey;
> The goose and fox, a friendly pair,
> Reposed beside the lamb and bear;

There horses stood for boys to ride;
Here boats were waiting for the tide,

While ships of war, with every sail
Unfurled, were anchored to a nail;
There soldiers stood in warlike bands;
And naked dolls held out their hands,
As though to urge the passers-by
To take them from the public eye.
This way and that, the Brownies ran;
To try the toys they soon began.

The Jack-in-box, so quick and strong,
With staring eyes and whiskers long,
Now o'er and o'er was set and sprung
Until the scalp was from it flung
And then they crammed him in
  his case,
With wig and night-cap in their
  place,
To give some customer a start
When next the jumper flew
  apart.
The trumpets, drums, and weap-
  ons bright
Soon filled them all with great
  delight.
Like troops preparing for their
  foes,
In single ranks and double
  rows,

They learned the arts of war, as told
By printed books and veterans old;
With swords of tin and guns of wood,
They wheeled about, and marched or stood,

And went through skirmish
    drill and all,
From room to room by bugle-
    call;
There Marathon and Waterloo
And Bunker Hill were fought
    anew;
And most of those in war array
At last went limping from the
    fray.
The music-box poured forth an
    air
That charmed the dullest spirits
    there,
Till, yielding to the pleasing sound,
They danced with dolls a lively round.

There fish were working tail and fin
In seas confined by wood and tin;
The canvas shark and rubber whale
Seemed ill content in dish or pail,
And leaping all obstructions o'er
Performed their antics on the floor.

Some found at marbles greatest fun,
And still they played, and still they won,
Until they claimed as winners, all
The shop could furnish, large and small.

More gave the singing tops no rest—
But kept them spinning at their best
Until some wonder strange and new
To other points attention drew.

The rocking-horse that wildly rose,
Now on its heels, now on its nose,
        Was forced to bear so great a load
        It seemed to founder on the road,
        Then tumble feebly to the floor,
        Never to lift a rocker more.

        No building in the country wide
        With more attractions was supplied,
        No shop or store throughout the land
        Could better suit the Brownie band.
        For when some flimsy toy gave way
                And 'round the room in pieces lay

143

'T was hardly missed in such a store,
With wonders fairly running o'er; .
To something else about the place
The happy Brownie turned his face,
And only feared the sun would call
Before he 'd had his sport with all.

Thus, through the shop in greatest glee,
They rattled 'round, the sights to see,
Till stars began to dwindle down,
And morning crept into the town.
And then, with all the speed they knew,
Away to forest shades they flew.